W9-BYY-235

# MAGICAL IDEAS

Written by
**Helen Murray**

Models by
**Emily Corl,**
**Rod Gillies,**
and **Kevin Hall**

# CONTENTS


8 Unicorn family
10 Enchanted forest
12 Fairy friends
14 Fairy village
16 Welcome fairies
17 Tooth fairy box
18 Mythical creatures
20 Fly away
22 Witching hour
23 Wise wizard
24 Wand workshop
26 Potions class
28 Amazing change!
29 Werewolf chums
30 Under the sea
32 Sea monsters
34 Genie in a lamp
35 Up, up, and away
36 Open sesame!
38 Lucky charms
40 Elf parade
41 Tetchy trolls

42 Snow queen
44 Silly giant
45 Magical goose
46 Friendly yeti
47 Search for Bigfoot
48 Once upon a time
50 Puppet show
52 Fairy-tale castles
54 Roaring dragons
56 Mischief makers
58 Candy village
60 Super heroes
62 Extraordinary animals
64 Marvelous vehicles
66 Over the rainbow
68 Go stargazing
70 Acknowledgments and Meet the builders

# UNICORN FAMILY

Create a whole family of colorful unicorns with magical horns. Why not add wings to make extra-special unicorns that can fly?

DADDY UNICORN

Brick with curved top forms nose
Angel wing piece
ALICORN (WINGED UNICORN)
Wings attach to plates with clips
Horn set into 1x1 round plate
Arch piece makes a colorful tail
1x1 round bricks for short legs
BABY UNICORN

# ENCHANTED FOREST

What was that noise? A tree? It can't be!
Build a forest where all is not as it seems.
Give your trees peeking eyes and
open mouths.

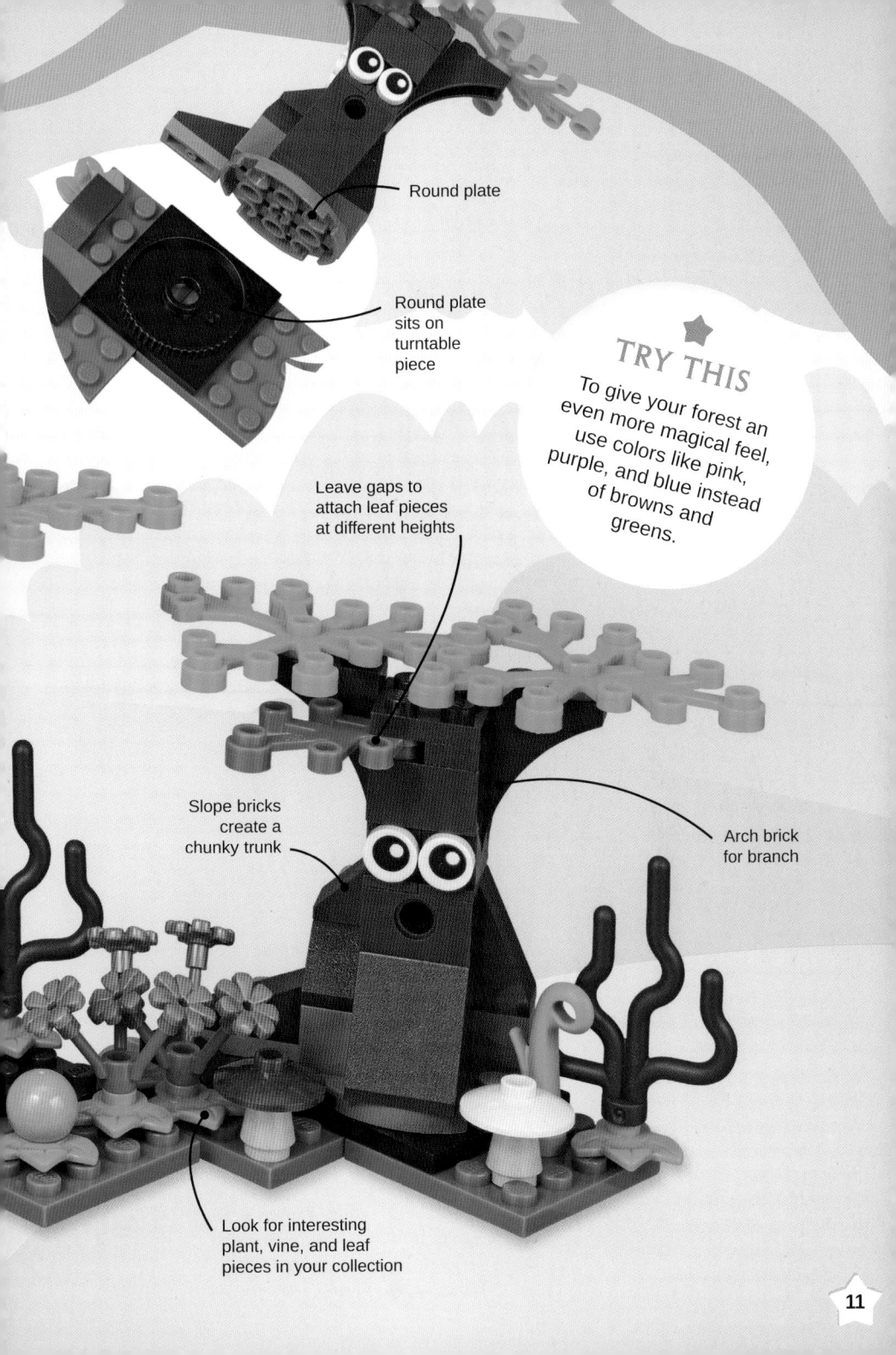
Round plate
Round plate sits on turntable piece
TRY THIS
To give your forest an even more magical feel, use colors like pink, purple, and blue instead of browns and greens.
Leave gaps to attach leaf pieces at different heights
Slope bricks create a chunky trunk
Arch brick for branch
Look for interesting plant, vine, and leaf pieces in your collection

# FAIRY FRIENDS

Do you believe in fairies? Make magical fairies with colorful wings and clothes. What adventures will your fairies get up to?

Wings attach to angle plate on fairy's back
Arm connects to body with LEGO® Technic pin
2x2 plate secures angled plates
TRY THIS
Use different colored angled plates for multicolored wings. If you have wing pieces in your LEGO® collection, you could use those, too.
Wings are four angled plates
Fluttering eyes
Tiny fairy's wings are two small angled plates
Cone makes a perfect fairy skirt
Two pink plates make up the fairy skirt

# FAIRY VILLAGE

Create beautiful homes for your fairy folk. Build an inviting fairy garden with tiny houses, or a cute cottage with a door for your little LEGO fairies to live inside.

**TRY THIS**

Build a pond or a bridge for your fairy garden. Why not build furniture for your fairy cottage, too? Make a tiny table, chair, or bed.

**FAIRY VILLAGE**

HMM... WHAT'S THE SPELL TO CLEAN MY ROOM?
LEGO Technic connector
LEGO Technic pin
This large flower makes the cottage look even smaller!
Chunky chimney
Keep your house hidden under some leaves
Round plate with hole for a window
Wand attaches to plate with clip
FAIRY COTTAGE
FAIRY

# WELCOME FAIRIES

Invite magic into your home by building a door so that fairies can enter from a magical land. You could leave notes and tiny gifts for your fairy visitors, too!

# TOOTH FAIRY BOX

Make the tooth fairy's job so much easier by creating a little box for your tooth to go inside. There might even be a surprise waiting for you in the morning!

# MYTHICAL CREATURES

There are many myths and legends about special animals who have a mix of fabulous features. Build a hippogriff, centaur, or faun—or why not make up your own fantastic beast?

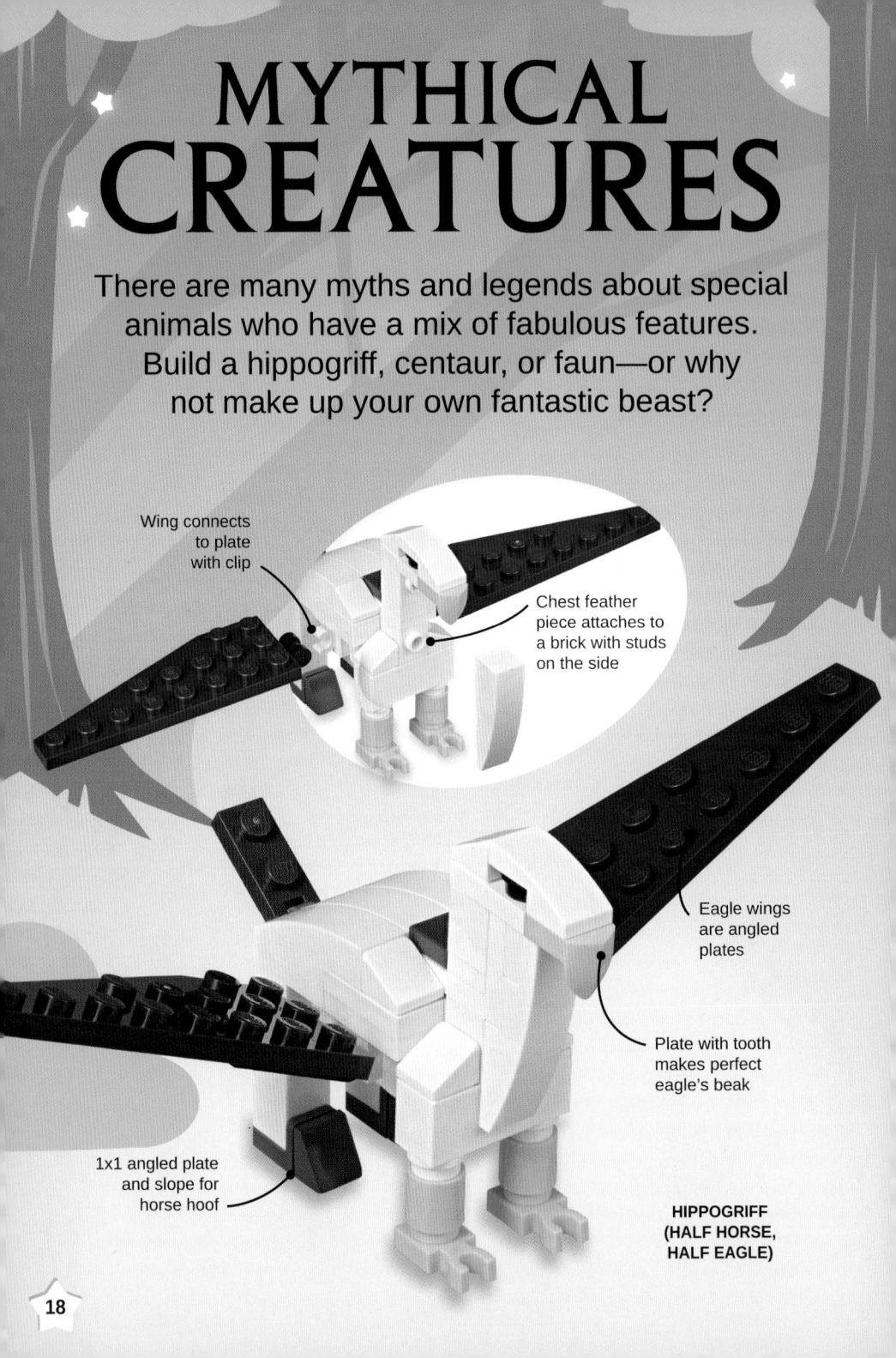


**HIPPOGRIFF (HALF HORSE, HALF EAGLE)**

SPECIAL BRICK

A 1x1 plate with clip is so handy. You can use it to attach something, but it also makes great features like hands, feet, and feathers.

# FLY AWAY

Go bird-watching—with a magical twist. Build birds with flame or lightning pieces, and you will have a phoenix that rises from the flames or a bird that shoots lightning!

**SPECIAL BRICK**

The wavy flame pieces make incredible phoenix wings. You could also use it for arms, blasters, or to decorate a blazing set of wheels!

PHOENIX

Transparent blue flame piece for crest
I'M SHOCKINGLY POWERFUL!
Lightning piece attaches to plate with clip
Chest feather is plate with tooth
Legs look like they are glowing!
LIGHTNING BIRD
WOAH! THAT IS SOME SPARROW!
If your bird has long, thin legs, pop it on a perch for extra stability.

WITCHING HOUR
Wait until it's dark outside and build a magical witch and her mischievous cat. Don't forget a pointy hat and broomstick!
HEE, HEE, HEE!
Cone makes a perfect pointy hat
Green bricks—for the classic witch look!
TRY THIS
What other animal helpers can you build with just a handful of bricks? How about a mouse or an owl?
Broomstick bricks attach above and below brick hand
HUBBLE BUBBLE ... HERE COMES TROUBLE!
Slopes form skirt shape
Just 12 pieces make up this cat!
Plate with tooth for the tail's tip
Yellow cone for brush

# WISE WIZARD

Create an enchanted magic-maker with a beard and wand. What spells will your wizard cast?

# WAND WORKSHOP

Cast a spell with a LEGO wand. Make a magician's wand, wizard's wand, or fairy wand—or see what other types of wands you can conjure up!

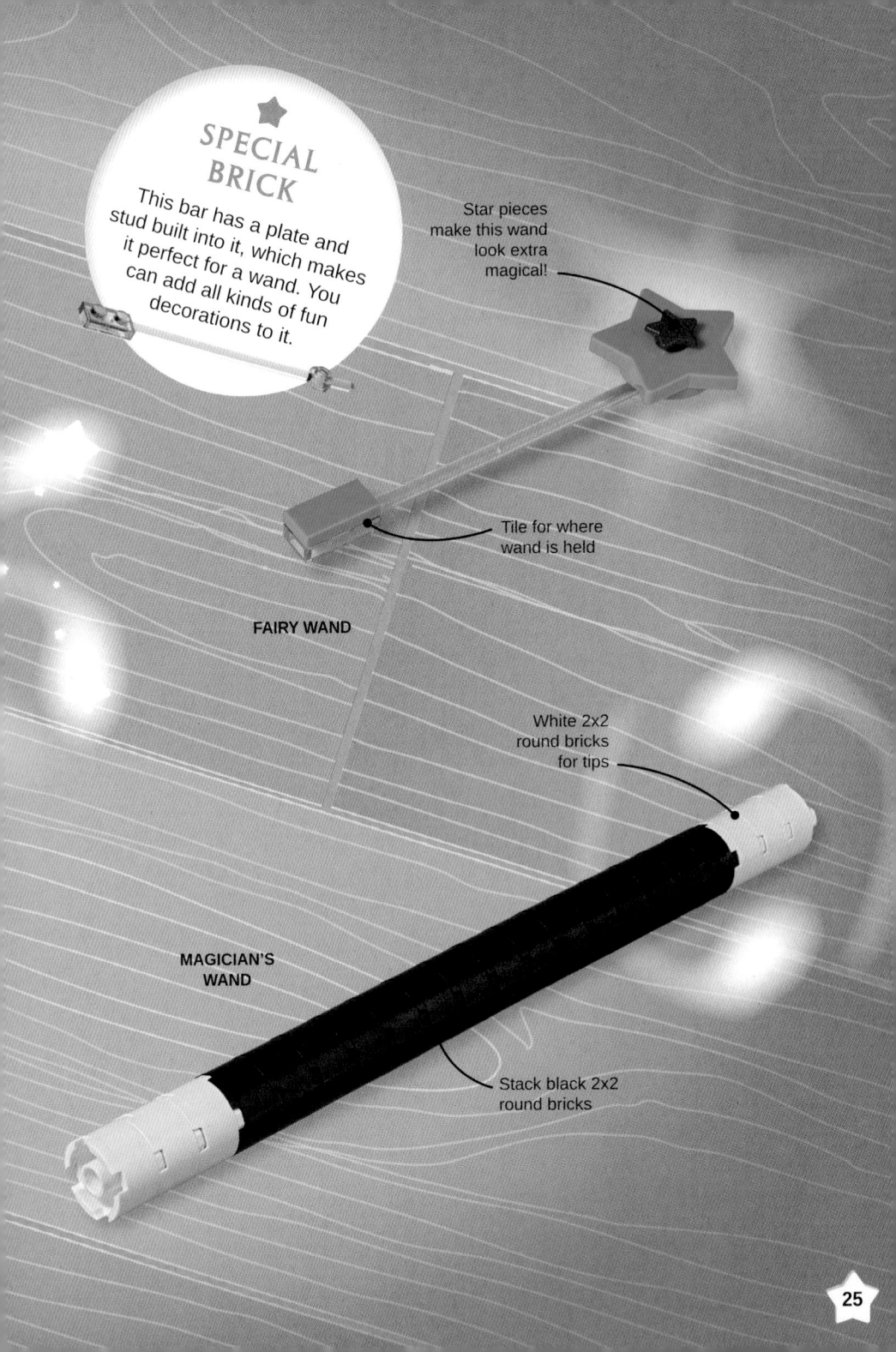
SPECIAL BRICK
This bar has a plate and stud built into it, which makes it perfect for a wand. You can add all kinds of fun decorations to it.
Star pieces make this wand look extra magical!
Tile for where wand is held
FAIRY WAND
White 2x2 round bricks for tips
MAGICIAN'S WAND
Stack black 2x2 round bricks

# POTIONS CLASS

Fizz! Bubble! Bang! Build a potions workshop and stir a bewitching brew, mix powerful potions, and practice your spells.

POTIONS WORKSHOP

**TOP TIP**

Look for small transparent pieces in your collection. Tiny 1x1 round bricks and slopes are ideal for miniature potion bottles.

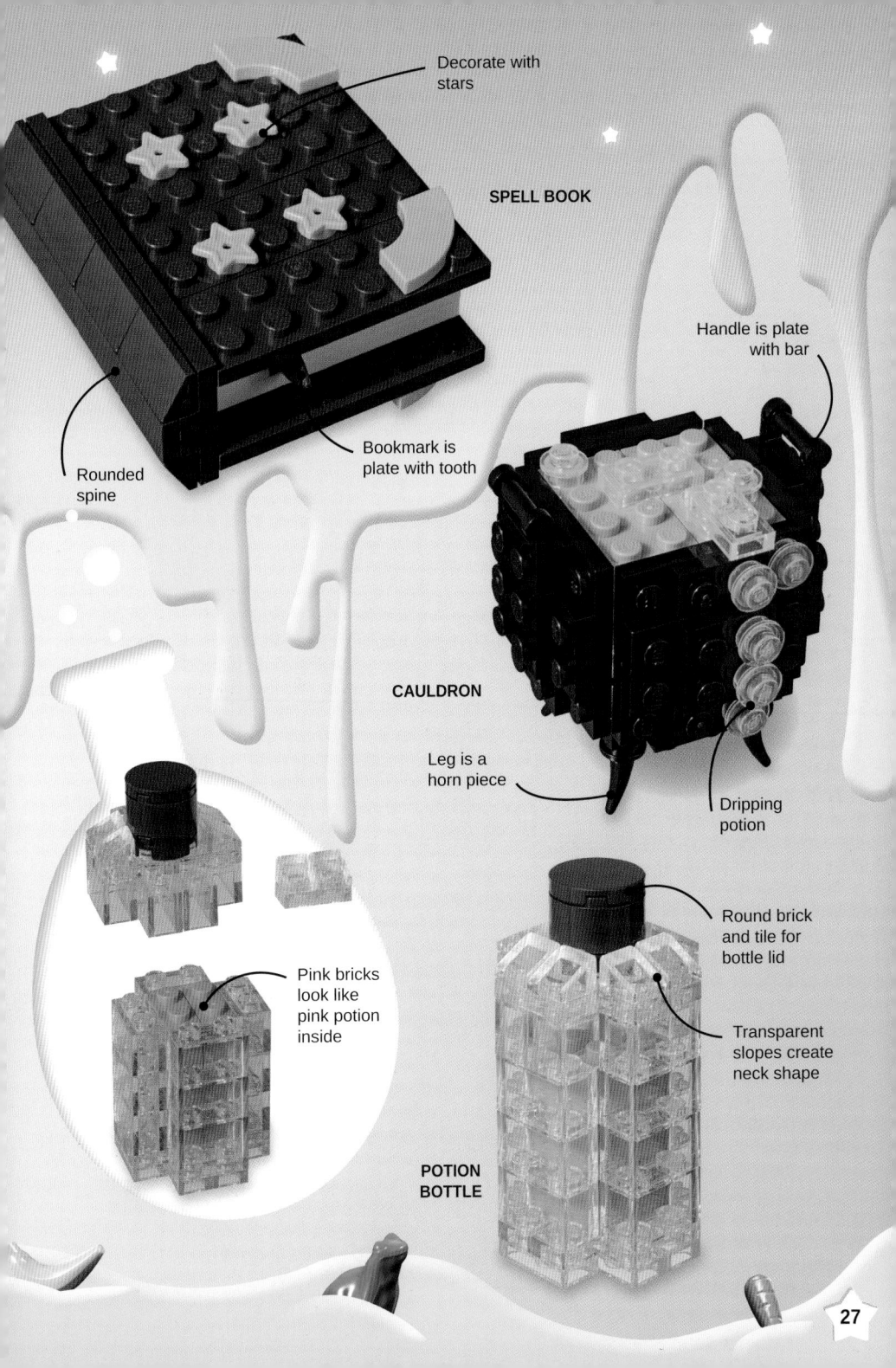
Decorate with stars
SPELL BOOK
Rounded spine
Bookmark is plate with tooth
Handle is plate with bar
CAULDRON
Leg is a horn piece
Dripping potion
Pink bricks look like pink potion inside
Round brick and tile for bottle lid
Transparent slopes create neck shape
POTION BOTTLE

# AMAZING CHANGE!

Wow your friends with a spellbinding transformation. Just use a LEGO® turntable piece for a touch of magic!

WEREWOLF CHUMS
Start building under the light of a full moon and you might just see your bricks transform into a pair of werewolf friends.
Pointy ear is 1x1 plate with horizontal tooth
ARRRROOOOO!
Human shorts from before the transformation
Fang is plate with vertical tooth
Slope bricks form legs and feet
Slope brick sits on top of slanted plates
1x2 plate with horizontal tooth for claws
SPECIAL BRICKS
A 1x1 plate with horizontal or vertical tooth can be used for all kinds of body parts. They make great teeth, ears, claws, beaks, and more.

# UNDER THE SEA

Create mermaids and mermen for magical adventures beneath the waves. Build a human top half and a dazzling tail for the bottom half.

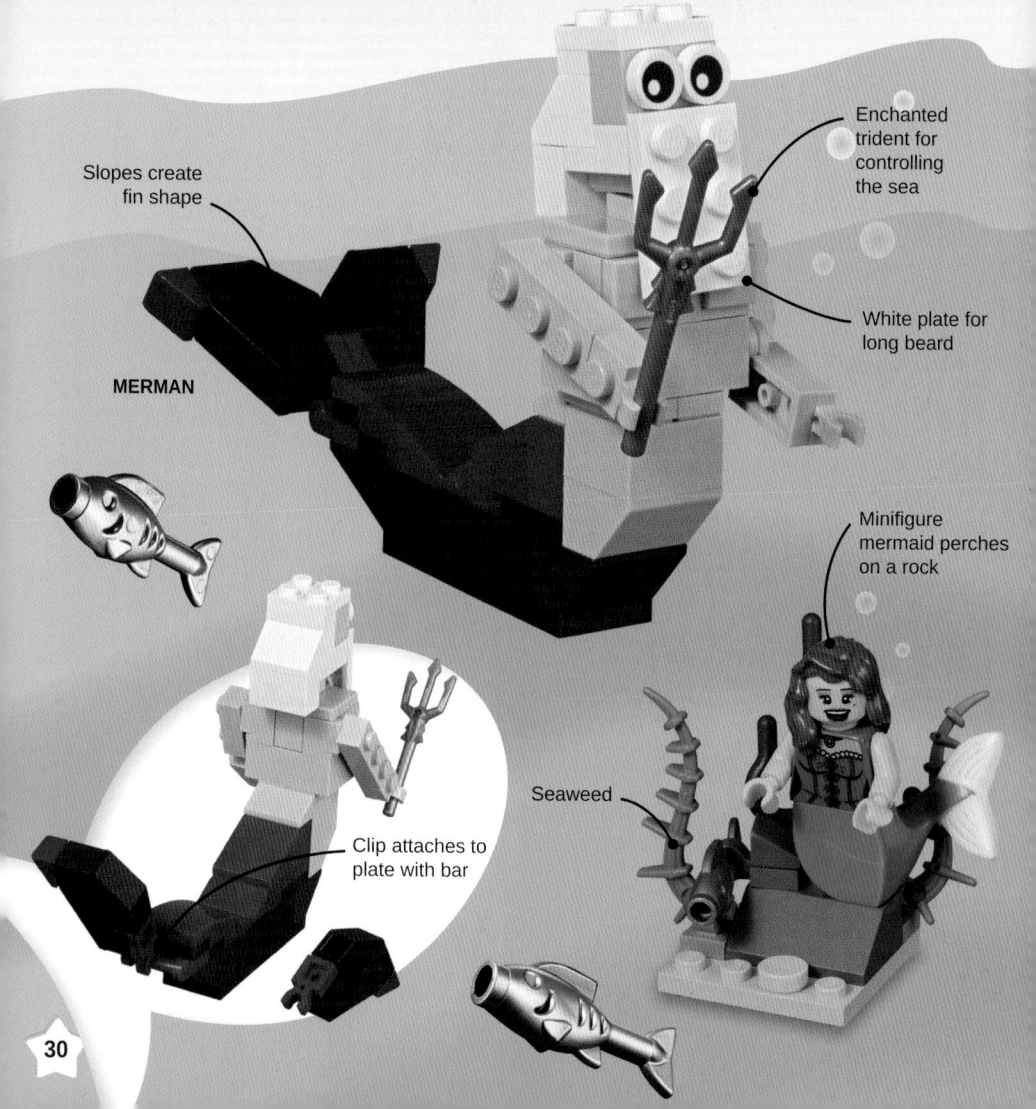

MERMAID
Long, flowing hair
Separate tail pokes out of the water
Pink mermaid top
I FEEL FIN-TASTIC TODAY!
TRY THIS
Build an underwater palace for your merpeople. Look for pieces that could work as treasure, shells, and plants to decorate it with.
Eye tile
1x1 slopes for fin tip
Plate with clip for hand
MERGIRL

# SEA MONSTERS

Build a mysterious monster of the deep blue sea. Perhaps yours will have a long, eel-like body or lots of wriggly, squiggly arms!

Short tentacle piece connects to brick with stud on side
Tentacle piece attaches to brick with hole
I NEVER SEE ANY UNUSUAL CREATURES...
Long tentacle
Main body is made from just six small bricks!
Angled eyes for a funny expression

KRAKEN

# GENIE IN A LAMP

Legend says that if you rub a magic lamp, a powerful genie will grant you three wishes. Why not try building your own? Remember: choose your wishes wisely!

# UP, UP, AND AWAY

Get your head in the clouds—and imagine the world from way up high. A LEGO magic carpet can take your minifigures anywhere!

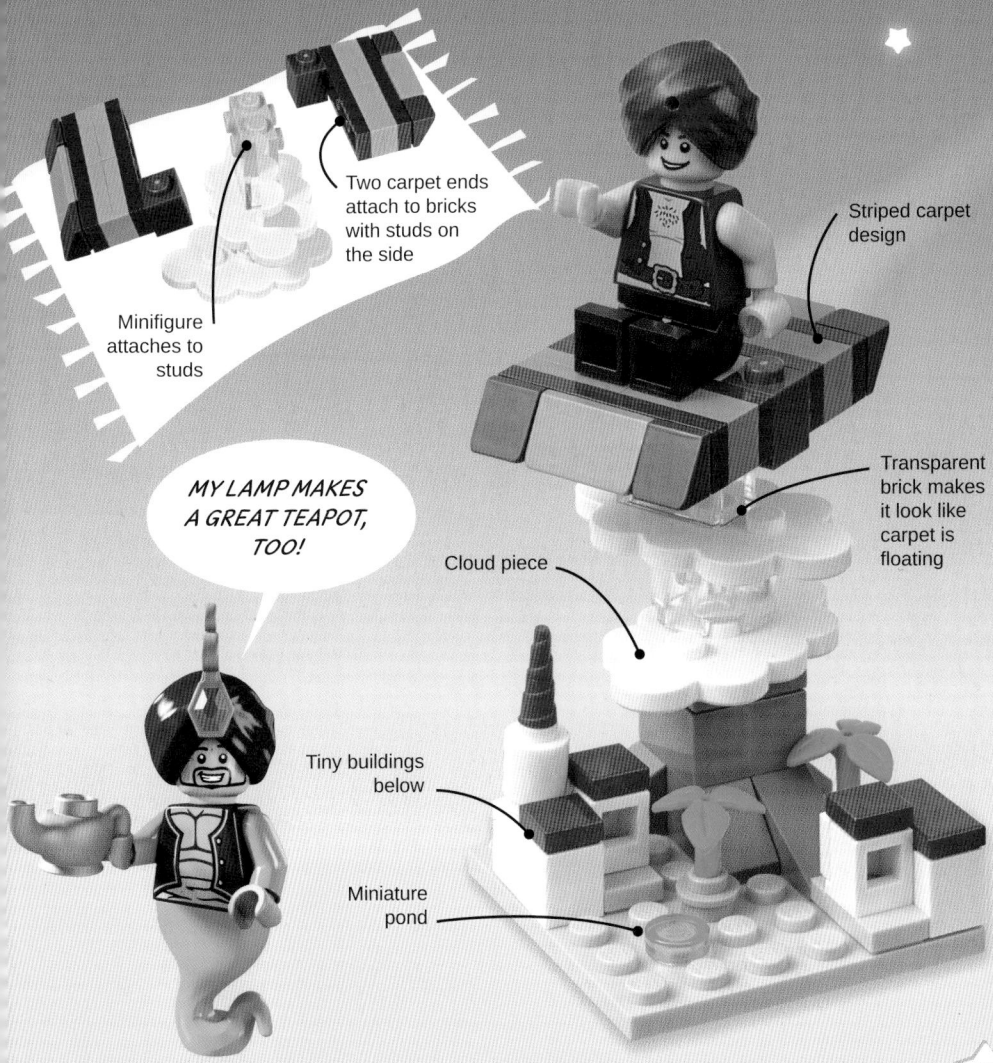

OPEN
SESAME!
Build a hidden cave with mountains of gold and precious jewels. Who knows? There might just be something magical inside!
Arch-shaped brick for entrance
Cave is hidden under plants
Chest is bursting with treasure
Stacks of coins are 1x1 round plates and tiles
CAVE
Use different types of gray bricks for an uneven, crumbling cave wall

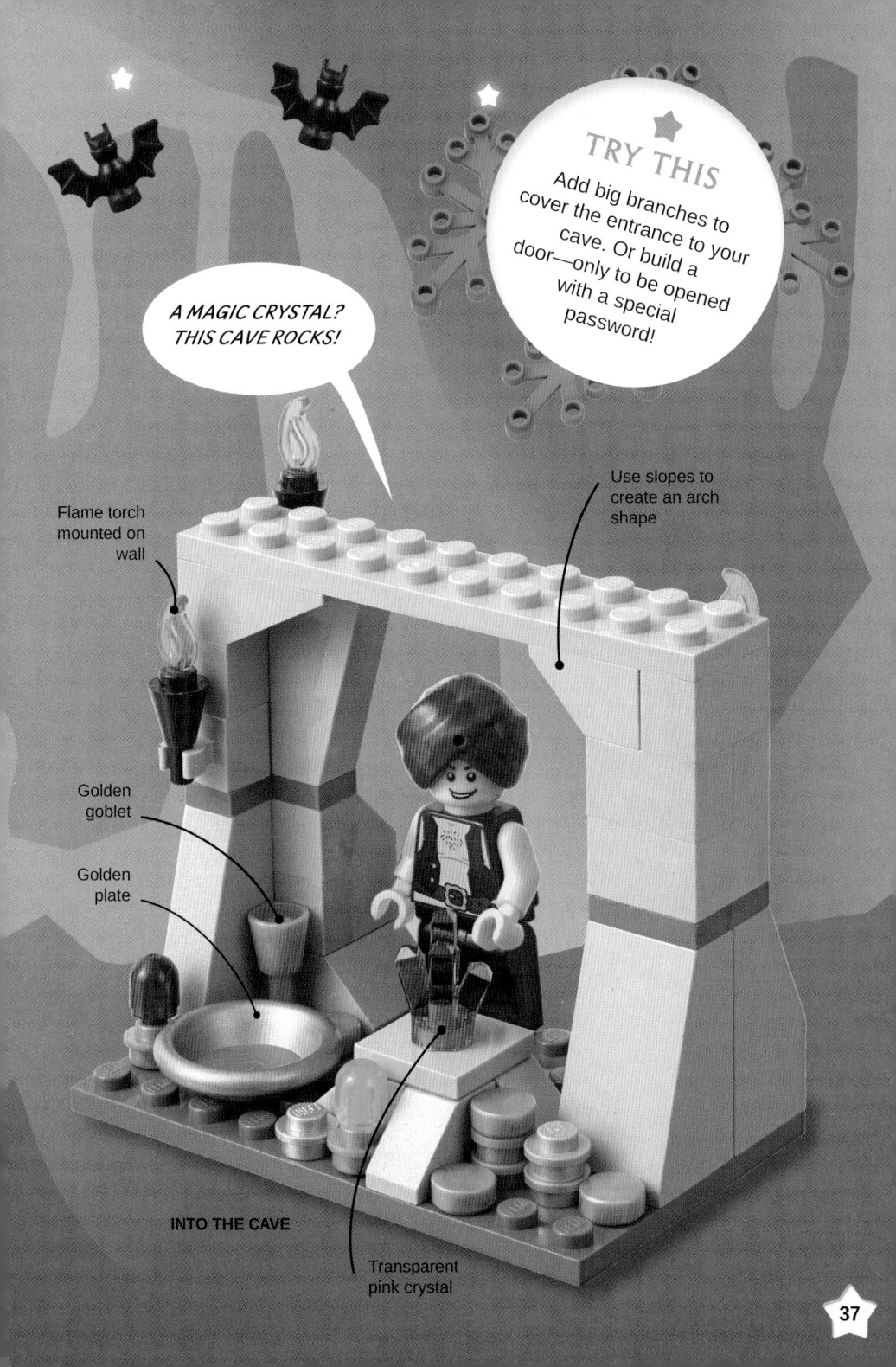
TRY THIS
Add big branches to cover the entrance to your cave. Or build a door—only to be opened with a special password!
A MAGIC CRYSTAL? THIS CAVE ROCKS!
Flame torch mounted on wall
Use slopes to create an arch shape
Golden goblet
Golden plate
Transparent pink crystal

# LUCKY CHARMS

Feeling lucky? It doesn't matter if you're not! Build yourself some good luck with a lucky LEGO four-leaf clover, die, or horseshoe.

FOUR-LEAF CLOVER

**SPECIAL BRICK**

This joyful heart plate also comes in red and dark pink. You'll feel lucky to have it in your collection!

*I HOPE I'M LUCKY ENOUGH TO FIND A POT OF GOLD!*

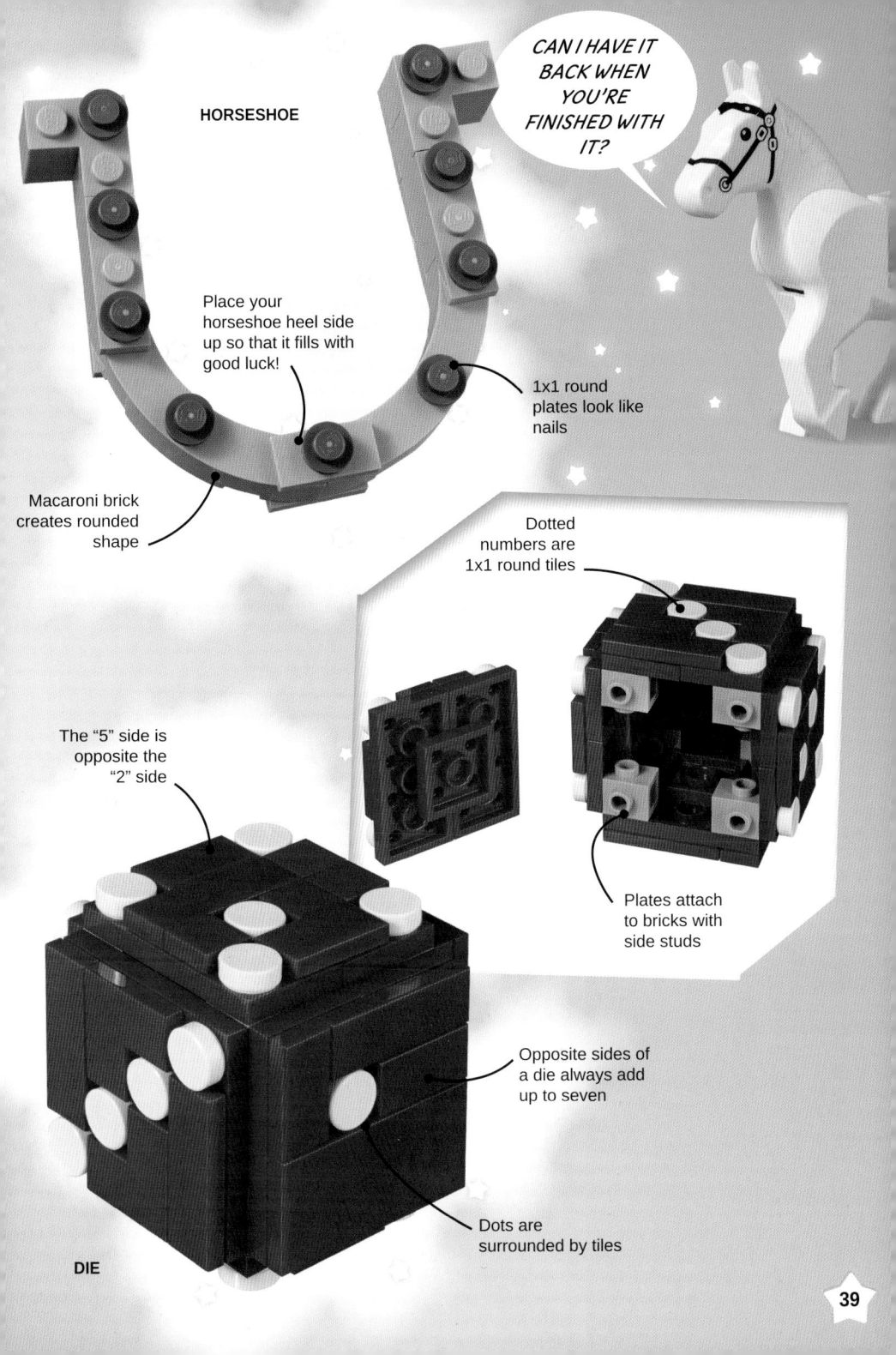
CAN I HAVE IT BACK WHEN YOU'RE FINISHED WITH IT?
HORSESHOE
Place your horseshoe heel side up so that it fills with good luck!
1x1 round plates look like nails
Macaroni brick creates rounded shape
Dotted numbers are 1x1 round tiles
Plates attach to bricks with side studs
The "5" side is opposite the "2" side
Opposite sides of a die always add up to seven
Dots are surrounded by tiles
DIE

# ELF PARADE

Build a gang of elves for adventures in enchanted lands. This mini elf looks like she's on her way to the North Pole to help Santa Claus!

# TETCHY TROLLS

Trolls like to hide in caves or under bridges, so they can be hard to spot. Why not build your own? Be warned, though—trolls can be grumpy!

# SNOW QUEEN

A snow queen can freeze anything! She can create magnificent ice sculptures with an icy blast of her hand. Build a snow queen and her glistening ice creations.

**TOP TIP**

When creating a small scene, start with a plate to build everything onto. A white or blue plate is perfect for an icy scene.

ICE THRONE

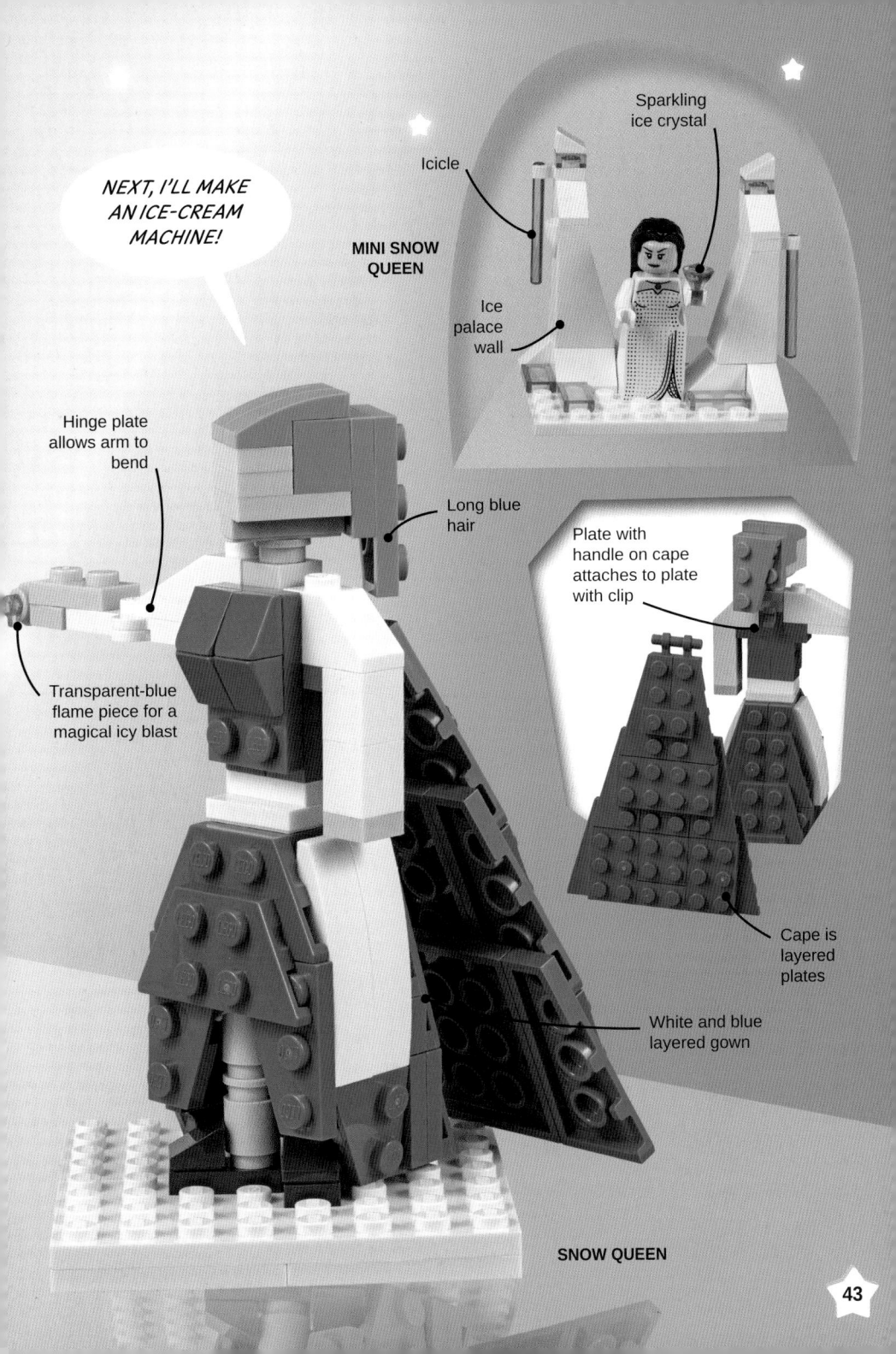
NEXT, I'LL MAKE AN ICE-CREAM MACHINE!
MINI SNOW QUEEN
Sparkling ice crystal
Icicle
Ice palace wall
Hinge plate allows arm to bend
Long blue hair
Plate with handle on cape attaches to plate with clip
Transparent-blue flame piece for a magical icy blast
Cape is layered plates
White and blue layered gown
SNOW QUEEN

# SILLY GIANT

Fee-fi-fo-fum ... I smell some teeny LEGO people below. Build a giant straight from a fairy tale. Decide whether you want yours to be fierce, friendly, or a bit silly!

# MAGICAL GOOSE

Build a goose—and have fun imagining what you would do if you had a goose that could lay golden eggs!

# FRIENDLY YETI

This yeti doesn't get to see many people because it lives up high in the remote mountains. Why don't you build another, so it can have a friend?

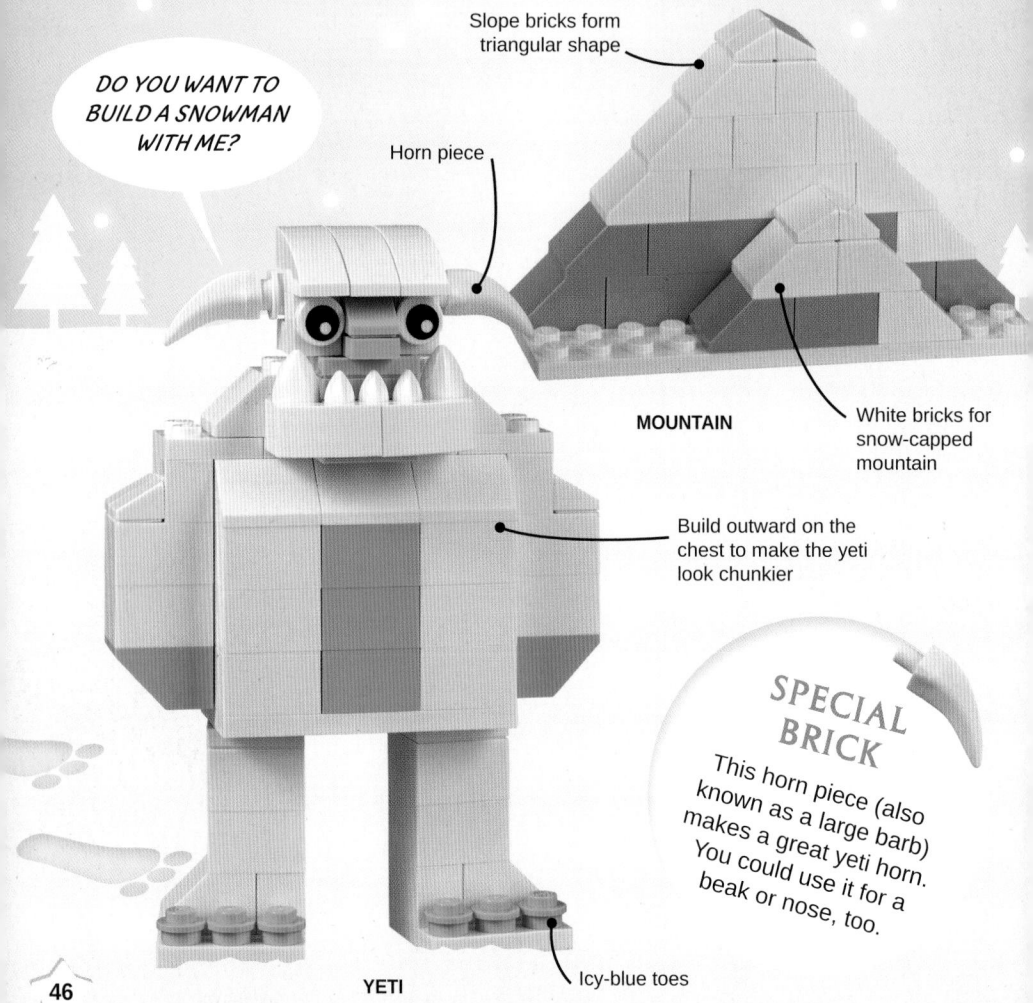


## SPECIAL BRICK

This horn piece (also known as a large barb) makes a great yeti horn. You could use it for a beak or nose, too.

# SEARCH FOR BIGFOOT

The mysterious Bigfoot is thought to live deep in the woods. These hairy creatures are so hard to track down that some people don't believe they exist. It might be easier to build your own!

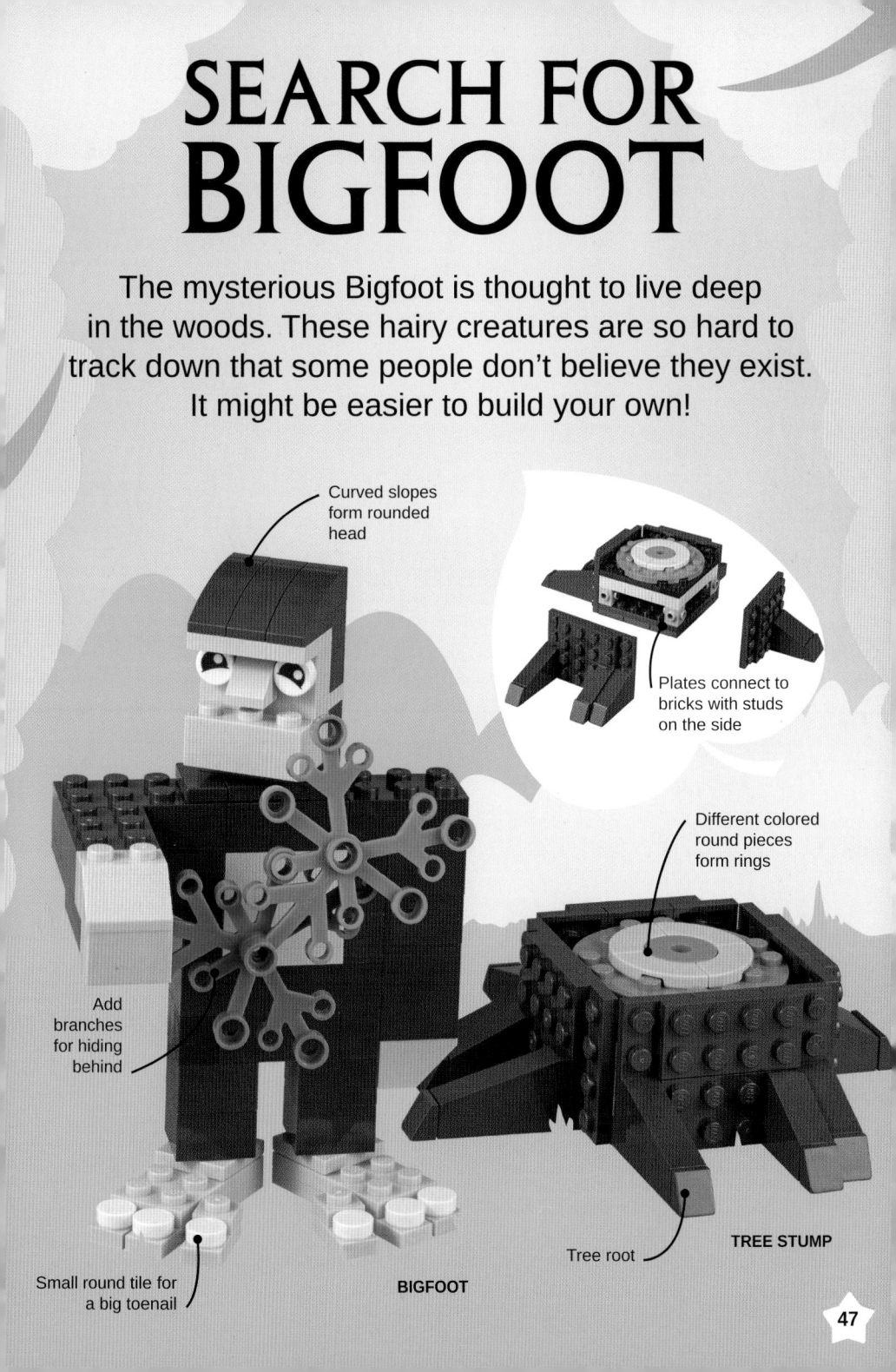

# ONCE UPON A TIME

"There was a brave princess who yearned for an adventure ..." Tell a magical fairy tale with your LEGO® bricks. What will your imagination dream up?

PART 1: THE FOREST OF FEAR

PART 2: THE HAUNTED HILLS

OH, THIS IS WHY IT'S CALLED THE STINKY SWAMP!
Swamp reed
Removing the minifigure's legs makes it look like she's wading
1x1 round plate for green bubble
PART 3: THE STINKY SWAMP
TOP TIP
Keep your scenes simple and small. Focus on a few key moments in the story.
Textured brick pattern
PHEW, MADE IT HOME IN TIME FOR DINNER!
Four scenes tell the story of the princess's adventure
Clean skirt after the dunk in the swamp
PART 4: BACK AT THE PALACE

# PUPPET SHOW

Build enchanting LEGO puppets and gather an audience for an unforgettable show. You control the puppets—and the magic! Why not make some wishes come true?

**TOP TIP**

Your puppet will need a stick. Use a long, narrow plate or a LEGO Technic axle that fits into a 2x2 round brick with axle hole.

Tiny arm attaches to brick with stud on the side
Sturdy helmet
PALACE GUARD
Round plate for chest armor
Angle plates form base of crown
Witchy green skin tone
Gray bricks for beard
Plate with clip for holding broom
WITCH
KING

# FAIRY-TALE CASTLES

You only need a handful of bricks to build magical mini LEGO castles with turrets and spires. Will you make yours look inviting or spooky?

GRAND CASTLE

Corner panel piece for high wall
MICRO CASTLE
Turret
TINY CASTLE
4x4 base plate
Slope bricks top the turrets
Build turrets at different heights
Colorful cones for fall trees
FOREST CASTLE
Dome with spire
Grille piece
WELCOME TO MY MINI QUEENDOM
Arch brick creates majestic entrance
MYSTICAL CASTLE

# ROARING DRAGONS

Some dragons are scary, but others are friendly and even bring good luck. What powers does your dragon have? You could add wings or fiery breath. Roooarrr!

SPLUTTER SPLUTTER! I'VE LOST MY PUFF!
Little yellow horns
Snout with teeth
Quarter-circle pieces for wings
CUTE DRAGON
Plates with clips attach to plate with bar
Wings attach with ball joints so they can be angled up and down
Long tail
Flame piece for fiery breath
FEARSOME DRAGON
Claws on wings

# MISCHIEF MAKERS

These colorful pranksters love to get up to no good! Have you lost a particular LEGO brick? Is your sock drawer mysteriously empty? It may well be this troublesome trio!

Head attaches to jumper plate
Hands are plates with clips
Large, flappy ears
Printed eye tile
BECAUSE IT WAS NOT PEELING WELL!
Upturned toes

# CANDY VILLAGE

Imagine living in a village that looks like your favorite foods! What will yours have? Fluffy marshmallow mountains? A birthday cake house? Lollipop trees? It all sounds good enough to eat!

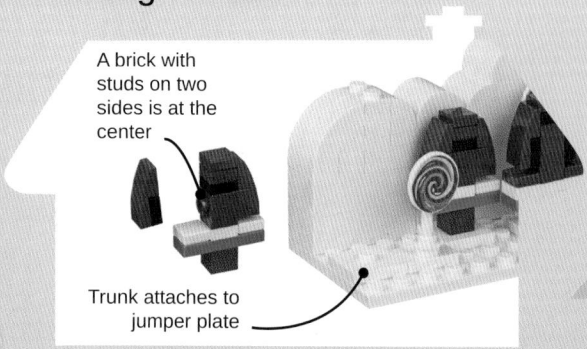

**MARSHMALLOW MOUNTAINS AND WATERMELON TREES**

SPECIAL BRICK
A printed swirly tile with clip on the back attaches to a bar to make a perfect lollipop tree.
Purple icing roof
Stacked round plates look like candy canes
GINGERBREAD HOUSE
Don't forget to add a candle!
Colorful icing
Brown bricks look like chocolate cake
Jumper plates for door
BIRTHDAY CAKE HOUSE
Cherry on top
Strawberry sauce made with pink plates
THERE'S NO PLACE LIKE A TASTY HOME!
Tan bricks for ice-cream cone
ICE-CREAM CONE HOUSE

# SUPER HEROES

These fantastic and fearless heroes use their magical powers to fight for good. Blue Bottle is super strong and The Green Fly can ... well, fly! What special powers will your super hero have?

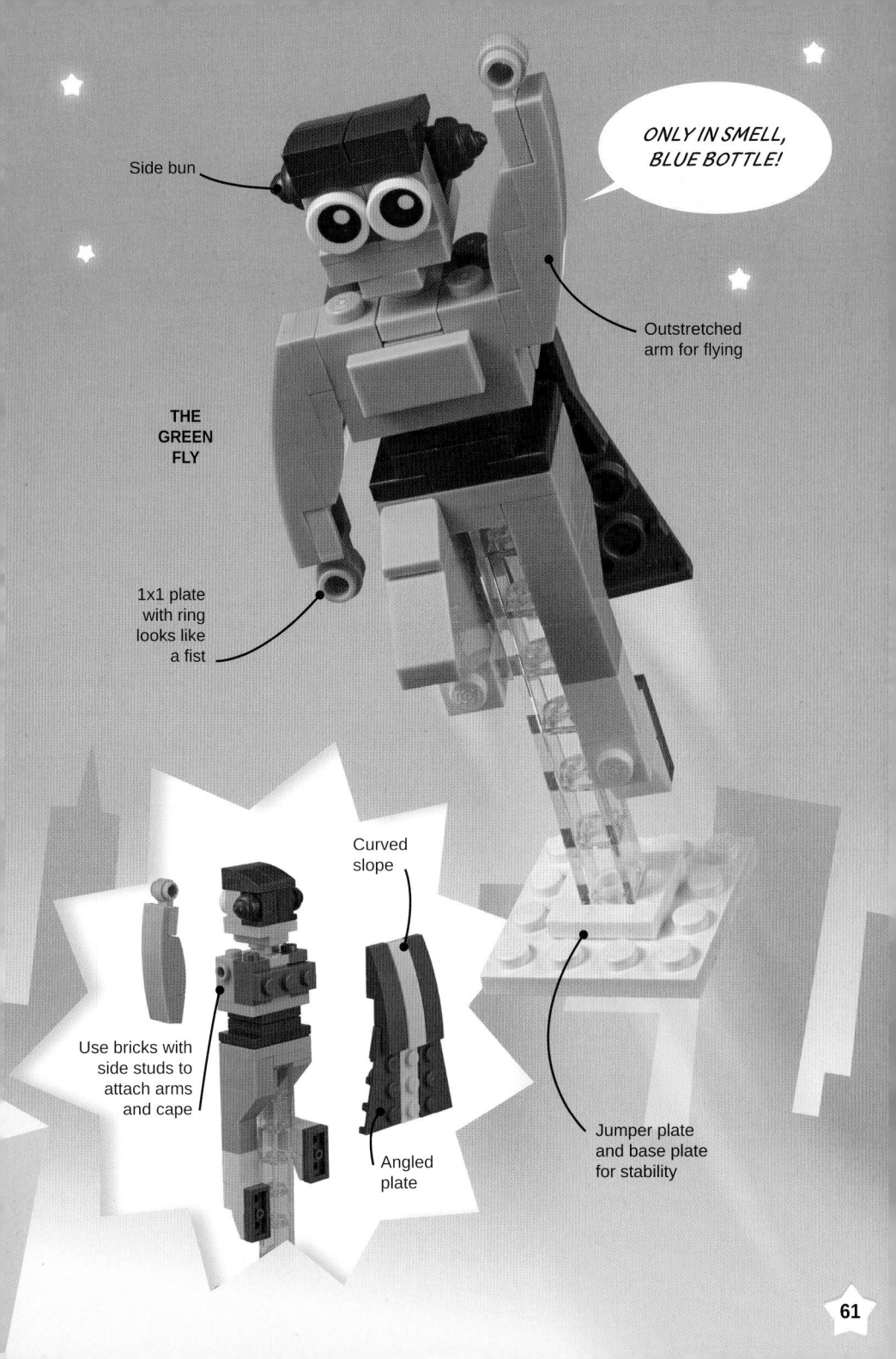
ONLY IN SMELL, BLUE BOTTLE!
Side bun
Outstretched arm for flying
THE GREEN FLY
1x1 plate with ring looks like a fist
Curved slope
Use bricks with side studs to attach arms and cape
Angled plate
Jumper plate and base plate for stability

# EXTRAORDINARY ANIMALS

Sprinkle a little magic to make ordinary animals extraordinary! Change the colors or add wings, horns, and tails where they wouldn't usually be to make a unique fantasy creature.

DRAGON-CAT

Plate attaches to bricks with side studs
Slope for ear
Studs look like curly wool
Multicolored fleece
WANT A CARROT? NO PROB-LLAMA
RAINBOW SHEEP
Unicorn horn
Pink and purple shell
TORTI-CORN
Sleepy eye
Short tortoise legs

# MARVELOUS VEHICLES

These elves get around in all kinds of magical ways! There's a spider walker that scuttles around on legs, a bike and a boat that can both also fly, and a submarine for underwater adventures.

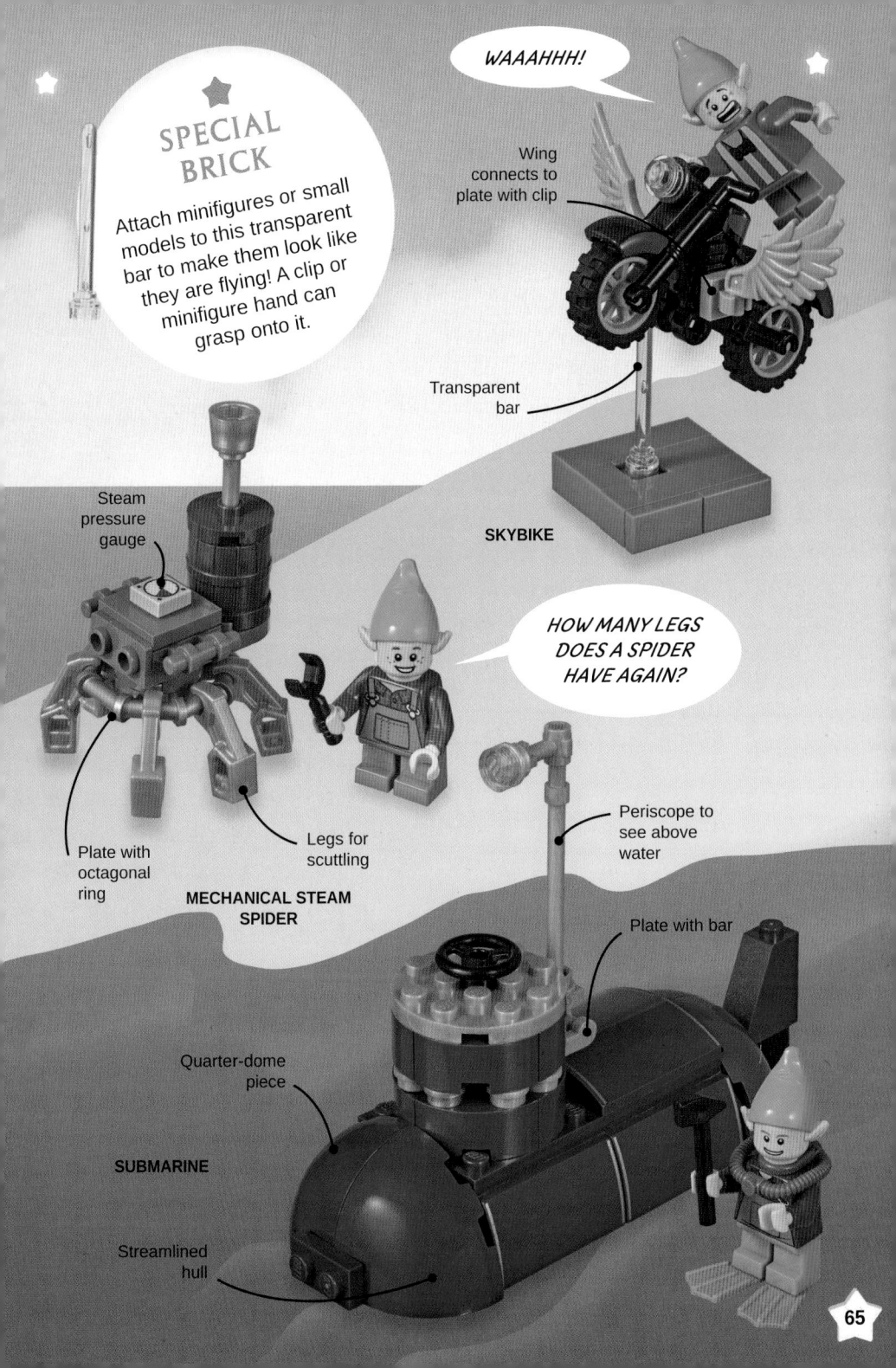
SPECIAL BRICK
Attach minifigures or small models to this transparent bar to make them look like they are flying! A clip or minifigure hand can grasp onto it.
WAAAHHH!
Wing connects to plate with clip
Transparent bar
SKYBIKE
Steam pressure gauge
HOW MANY LEGS DOES A SPIDER HAVE AGAIN?
Plate with octagonal ring
Legs for scuttling
MECHANICAL STEAM SPIDER
Periscope to see above water
Plate with bar
Quarter-dome piece
SUBMARINE
Streamlined hull

# OVER THE RAINBOW

When it is both sunny and rainy, a rainbow appears … as if by magic! Will your LEGO® rainbow have a pot of gold at the end?

## TRY THIS

You could build a flat, two-dimensional rainbow onto a base plate. Place each brick directly on the base plate. Stagger the bricks like a staircase as you arrange them in a semicircle shape.

Two layers of small plates make up each layer of color
Angle the plates to make a quarter-circle shape
1x1 round bricks for gold coins
Pot handle is plate with bar
RAINBOW WITH POT OF GOLD
A POT OF GOLDEN HONEY? HOORAY!
White base plate blends in with clouds

# GO STARGAZING

Can you spot a familiar shape in the stars of the night sky? These patterns of sparkling stars are called constellations. Map the magical night sky with your LEGO bricks.

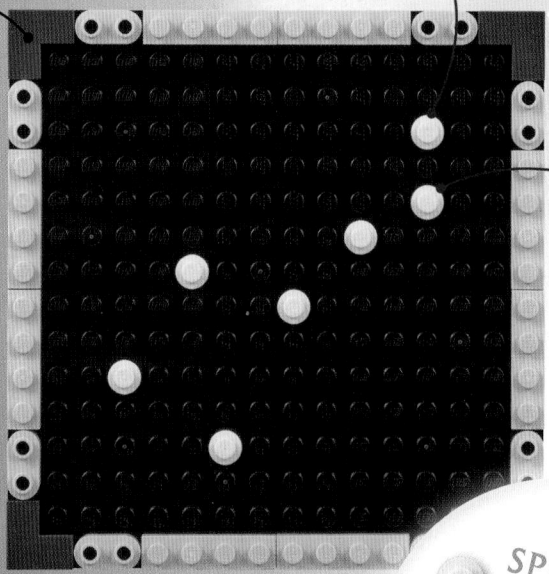


**THE BIG DIPPER (ALSO KNOWN AS THE PLOW)**

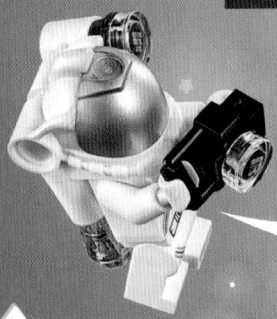

*WOW, THAT'S OUT OF THIS WORLD!*

**SPECIAL BRICK**

Place these glow-in-the-dark 1x1 round plates in lots of light before you put them in the dark—and watch your constellations glow!

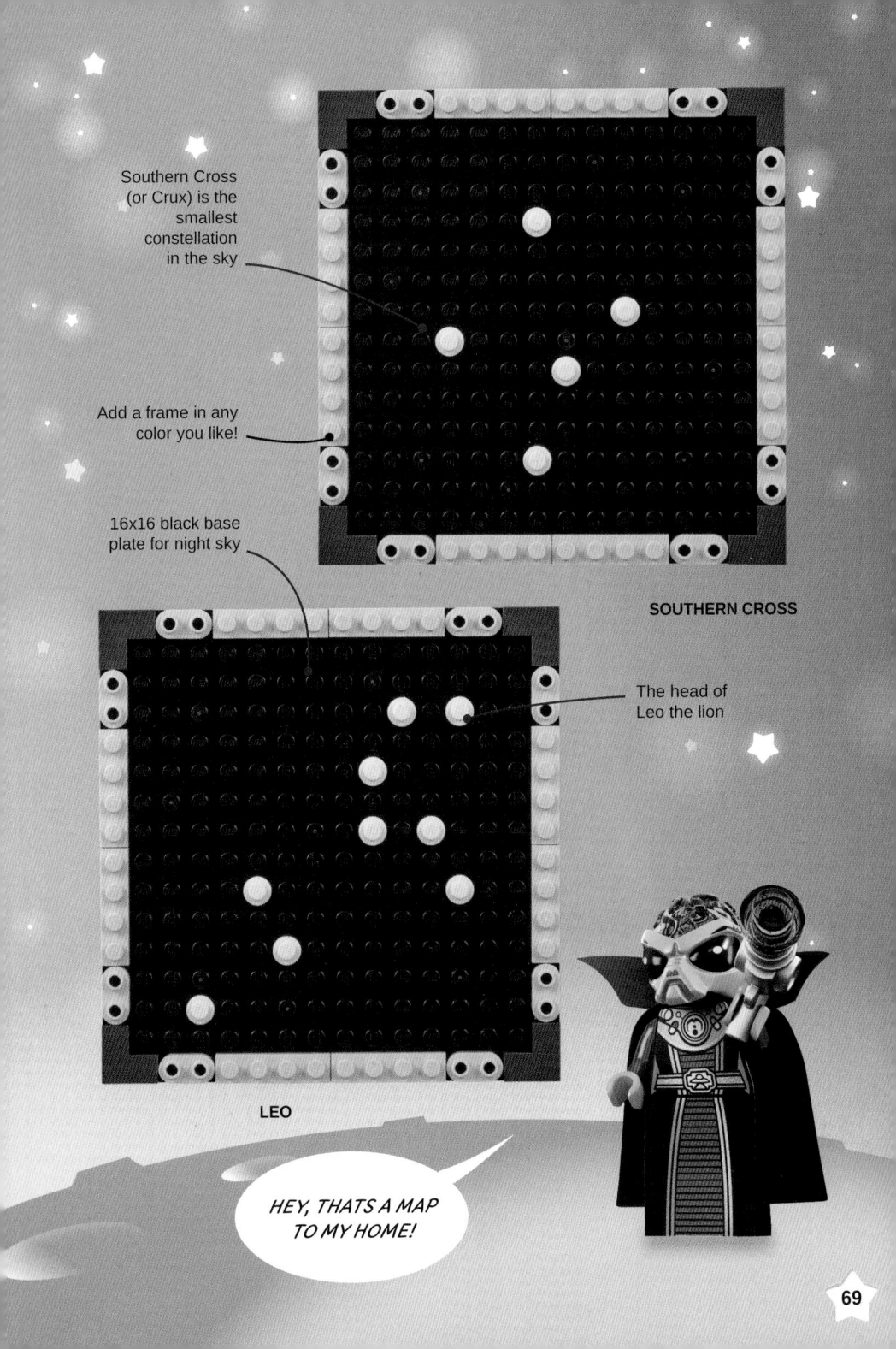
Southern Cross (or Crux) is the smallest constellation in the sky
Add a frame in any color you like!
16x16 black base plate for night sky
SOUTHERN CROSS
The head of Leo the lion
LEO
HEY, THATS A MAP TO MY HOME!

**Senior Editor** Helen Murray
**Senior Designer** Guy Harvey
**Senior Production Editor** Marc Staples
**Senior Production Controller** Louise Daly
**Managing Editor** Paula Regan
**Managing Art Editor** Jo Connor
**Publishing Director** Mark Searle
**Model Photography** Gary Ombler

**Models designed and created by**
Emily Corl, Rod Gillies, and Kevin Hall

Dorling Kindersley would like to thank: Randi Sørensen, Heidi K. Jensen, Paul Hansford, Martin Leighton Lindhardt, Nina Koopmann, Charlotte Neidhardt, and Torben Vad Nissen at the LEGO Group; Sam Bartlett for initial design work; Julia March for proofreading, and Megan Douglass for Americanizing.

First American Edition, 2021
Published in the United States by DK Publishing
1450 Broadway, Suite 801, New York, New York 10018

Page design copyright ©2021 Dorling Kindersley Limited
DK, a Division of Penguin Random House LLC
21 22 23 24 25 10 9 8 7 6 5 4 3 2 1
001–321738–Aug/2021

LEGO, the LEGO logo, the Minifigure, and the Brick and Knob configurations are trademarks and/or copyrights of the LEGO Group.
© 2021 The LEGO Group. All rights reserved.

Manufactured by Dorling Kindersley, One Embassy Gardens, 8 Viaduct Gardens, London SW11 7BW, under license from the LEGO Group.

All rights reserved. Without limiting the rights under the copyright reserved above, no part of this publication may be reproduced, stored in, or introduced into a retrieval system, or transmitted, in any form, or by any means (electronic, mechanical, photocopying, recording, or otherwise), without the prior written permission of the copyright owner.
Published in Great Britain by
Dorling Kindersley Limited.

A catalog record for this book is available from the Library of Congress.

ISBN 978-0-7440-2784-6

Printed and bound in China

For the curious

www.dk.com

www.LEGO.com

FSC www.fsc.org MIX Paper from responsible sources FSC™ C018179

This book was made with Forest Stewardship Council™ certified paper—one small step in DK's commitment to a sustainable future.

## MEET THE BUILDERS

### EMILY CORL

Emily is a professional LEGO® brick artist and builder. She loves the fairy door model as she can imagine knocking on the door and a little fairy opening it!

### ROD GILLIES

Rod is a LEGO fan who has always loved fantasy and adventure stories, and LEGO® Castle. His favorite models to build were the magical puppet show characters.

### KEVIN HALL

Kevin runs his own company creating LEGO models. He had great fun designing different styles of fairy-tale castles at a micro scale. His top tip is to never stop building!